Zoë
and the Dragon

For Alfred and Stephanie

MYRIAD BOOKS LIMITED
35 Bishopsthorpe Road, London SE26 4PA

First published in 2003 by
PICCADILLY PRESS LIMITED
5 Castle Road, London NW1 8PR
www.piccadillypress.co.uk

ISBN 1 905606 91 5
EAN 9 781905 606 917

Designed by Louise Millar

Printed in China

Zoë
and the Dragon

Jane Andrews

MYRIAD BOOKS LIMITED

At last, everything looked bright and beautiful in the
Fairy Queen's garden again. Last week the naughty elves had
picked every single flower in the garden, which had made the
Fairy Queen *very* angry. But, with the help of the fairies, now
new flowers were blooming again.
Zoë and Pip painted signs that said "No Elves" and posted
them throughout the garden.

Just as they were about to leave for the day, they heard some quiet sobbing.

"It's coming from behind that flower pot," said Zoë.

Both fairies flew over to get a better look.

"Oh dear, poor dragon," said Pip. "Whatever is the matter?"

The dragon told the fairies how everyone laughed at him because he wasn't scary.

"The animals in the wood giggle, and the elves just fall about laughing," he said between sobs. "I can't even breathe fire." Zoë and Pip comforted him and promised they would come back and check on him the next morning.

But that night the elves came back to the garden. They paid no attention to the "No Elves" signs. They picked nearly every flower. They made mud pies and threw them everywhere. They broke the branches off trees and bushes . . . They were naughtier than ever!

And the dragon just hid helplessly in a corner.

The next morning, the Fairy Queen was furious. She was red with rage.

Her garden was a complete and utter mess!

So she called a meeting later that morning. Everyone came and Zoë and Pip brought the dragon.

"This is an emergency!" the Queen announced. "We need a guard for the garden." Then she looked around at everyone and spotted the dragon. "*You* will be the new guard!"

The dragon gulped. He was too frightened to speak.
But Zoë whispered in his ear, "Don't worry, Pip and I have
a plan."

The fairies led the dragon deep into the castle. He followed them up long, winding staircases, through corridors, around corners . . . until eventually they came to a door.

The door opened into a room full of costumes and party clothes.

The three of them had a wonderful time dressing up in different costumes.

Then Zoë picked out a cloak, some gloves and a hat, and the fairies set to work.

Pip cut some holes in the cloak for the dragon's eyes, ears, arms and wings.

"These will make you look *really* scary," said Zoë.

The two fairies fluttered around the dragon, helping him dress. And when they finished, they steered him towards the mirror . . .

"WOW!" said the three of them together. The dragon hardly recognised himself.

Later that night Zoë and Pip hid in the garden with the dragon and waited for the elves to appear. Soon they could see the naughty little elves sneaking out from their hiding places. "Now!" shouted Zoë and Pip.

The dragon took a deep breath and started to run, flapping his arms.

"Aaaarrgh! A dragon!" shrieked the elves, running as fast as they could to get out of the garden.

But just as the last of the elves reached the hedge, the dragon suddenly stumbled and stepped on to his cloak, pulling it off!

"Oh no!" whispered Zoë.
There was silence as the dragon looked at the elves, and the elves looked back at the dragon. Then the dragon took a very long, deep breath . . .

"*RRROAR!!!*" thundered the dragon, and a huge jet of fire blew straight over the heads of the elves, singeing their hats. This surprised the dragon, almost as much as it surprised everybody else!

"Wow!" cheered Zoë, "You really are fierce!"

News of the dragon's triumph spread fast.
The next morning, the Fairy Queen congratulated him. "With
a fierce and brave dragon like you," she said, "my garden
is safe forever from those naughty elves."
And the dragon felt very proud of himself, and of his friends.